Wedding Day
Disaster

Wedding Day
Disaster

Rose Inserra

Illustrated by Trish Hill

 sundance

Published by
Sundance Publishing
234 Taylor Street
Littleton, MA 01460

Copyright © text Rose Inserra
Copyright © illustrations Trish Hill
Project commissioned and managed by
Lorraine Bambrough-Kelly, The Writer's Style
Designed by Cath Lindsey/design rescue

First published 1998 by
Addison Wesley Longman Australia Pty Limited
95 Coventry Street
South Melbourne 3205 Australia
Exclusive United States Distribution: Sundance Publishing

ISBN 0-7608-3288-9

Print

25210

Contents

Chapter 1

A Case of Chicken Pox

It came as no surprise to Patty that her twin sister, Penny, had been chosen to be bridesmaid at Cousin Fiona's wedding.

"If you'd try to talk to people instead of sitting in front of that computer all the time, you'd be popular, too," Penny told her sister.

"You're such a show-off," Patty replied angrily. "You love being the center of attention."

"Who cares if I'm not a stupid bridesmaid?" Patty thought. "I'm glad I'm not the center of attention."

Patty hated attention. She became tongue-tied and blushed when she had to read aloud or answer a question in class. It was better to talk to the computer. She was a whiz on the Internet. But sometimes she felt a bit lonely and wished she could be popular like her twin sister.

The morning before Cousin Fiona's wedding, an extraordinary thing happened. Patty's twin sister, Penny, woke up with a rash. It was no ordinary rash—it was chicken pox.

"Why did I have to get chicken pox?" wailed Penny, as she sniffed into a tissue.

Patty leaned close to her sister. "Here, give me some spots. Then I won't have to go to the wedding at all. I *hate* weddings."

"It's lucky you've had chicken pox, Patty,"
Mom announced. "You can take Penny's
place at the wedding as bridesmaid."

Patty looked at her mother in horror. "No way! I'll stay home with Dad and Penny. Please, Mom," she begged.

But Mom couldn't be swayed. No amount of bribing, moaning, and complaining could convince her to change her mind.

"You're going to be bridesmaid at your cousin's wedding, and that's that!" Mom ordered, as she grabbed two suitcases from the closet and began to pack.

Chapter 2

A Hiccup or Two

The ride to Cousin Fiona's farm was long and tiring. Patty was so bored that she counted sheep and horses to help pass the time on the three-hour drive.

When they finally arrived, Cousin Fiona was too nervous to worry about Patty taking Penny's place as bridesmaid. Patty thought Cousin Fiona looked like a huge marshmallow, with her frothy white dress and long gauzy veil.

Patty hated being fussed over. Her head itched, and the lace around her collar choked her. The hot weather didn't help. She felt clammy and hot—even her flowers were starting to droop.

"Now, remember, the bride's always supposed to be late to the church!" someone yelled, as they started off.

Soon the farmhouse was deserted.
Everyone had left except Patty, Cousin
Fiona, and Uncle Stuart. The sky had
become overcast, and it was very hot and
humid. The air was still—even the flies had
stopped buzzing.

Patty had a sinking feeling that something was about to happen—something bad.

Patty was right. Uncle Stuart accidentally stepped on the train of Cousin Fiona's wedding dress and ripped it!

Cousin Fiona wailed, "How could you do such a careless thing?"

She rushed back inside the house and ordered Patty to go get a needle and thread.

"That should do it," Patty said fifteen minutes later, when the dress was finally back in one piece.

Patty wished she had the courage to tell Fiona that her dress looked better without the frilly train. Now it looked particularly bad, because it was sewn unevenly, a little like hundreds of scrunched-up caterpillars.

"Let's go," Cousin Fiona said excitedly.

But disaster was to strike yet again. When Uncle Stuart tried to start the car . . . *Choke . . . Splutter . . . Cough!*

"Oh, no!" Cousin Fiona screamed. "Can you fix it quickly, Dad?"

Uncle Stuart was convinced that he could fix it quickly. He opened the hood and pulled, rubbed, and twisted. Finally, he kicked the car, but still nothing happened.

When Uncle Stuart called the local mechanic, nobody was there. When he called his neighbor, there was nobody home. Even the police station wasn't answering. Everyone was on their way to the wedding.

In a town of 236 people, there was not one person at home. *Everyone* had been invited to the wedding.

25

"It looks like we'll have to use the pickup," said Uncle Stuart, pointing to the old truck.

The ancient vehicle was caked with layers of red dirt. Inside, dirt, straw, feathers, fur, and other disgusting blobs covered the floor and seat.

Cousin Fiona blinked away her tears. "If the pickup is the only way to get to the church, then we'd better take it," she said, as she wiped the seat with a cloth.

Inside the pickup, Patty was sandwiched between her cousin and uncle. Poor Patty was so squeezed that she could hardly breathe. The bride's dress, which had once looked like a marshmallow, now looked like a squashed mushroom.

Chapter 3

Disaster Strikes Again

For six miles the pickup rocked and bounced along the rough road. Then *ker . . . plunk . . . ker . . . plunk . . . plunk* sounds joined the rocking and bouncing.

"We'd better pull over," Uncle Stuart suggested. "Something's not right."

Cousin Fiona looked at Patty miserably. They both thought the same thing—not another disaster!

"Looks like a flat tire," Uncle Stuart reported after his inspection. "Everyone out."

"Change the tire quickly!" said Cousin Fiona.

"Can't. The spare's at home with a hole in it," replied her father.

Patty dragged herself out of the pickup and sat on a log by the side of the road. There was no phone, nobody on the road, and the bride looked sad enough to be going to a funeral.

Patty wished she could help. She had to think of a plan. And fast . . .

"Are there horses on that farm?" Patty asked excitedly, pointing to the white fence in the distance.

They looked at her strangely at first.

"We can't really use them for riding. They're Bob Brown's old nags. They've been retired because they're so old," said Cousin Fiona.

There was silence. Patty was disappointed. Her only chance to help seemed lost. "Why don't we try? It would be better to get to the church late, instead of never," she said.

Uncle Stuart smiled and patted Patty on the shoulder. "Good idea, Penny, I mean Patty."

Cousin Fiona reluctantly agreed.

Patty had never been on a horse before, but she had watched a movie about horseback riding. With trembling knees, she straddled the horse and prepared herself for another exhausting six-mile journey.

Patty's horse was a gray one, called Mischief. It was the slowest horse she had ever seen. It certainly had no mischief whatsoever left in it!

The sun was out again, and its sizzling rays stung them as they rode. Flies swarmed around them, sticking onto their sweaty faces.

The flowers in the bouquets had wilted, and many of the petals had blown away in the breeze. Fiona's hair was now a frizzy halo under her fly-covered veil.

Still another three miles to go, and not a single car in sight. Or a bicycle. Or a motorcycle.

Cousin Fiona smiled. For the first time, she really seemed to notice Patty, who hadn't complained once, even though her whole body was sore and her skin looked like a lobster's.

Patty thought about Penny and how she would have behaved. Penny would have refused to go anywhere near a horse. And she would have sulked and complained about everything—the heat, the flies, the smells.

The sun suddenly disappeared. The clouds clung together to form a gray blanket.

A flash of lightning.

A rumble of thunder.

And then huge raindrops pelted down on them.

There was no point in riding on in such dangerous conditions. The road was a curtain of mist, and its surface had become slippery.

"There's an old shed just ahead!" Uncle Stuart yelled. "Follow me!"

Patty was very frightened. The rain was stinging her face, and she worried that Mischief might stumble on the slippery road.

What a disastrous day! They were wet and miserable and dirty. *And* they were late for the wedding. But at least they were safe in the old shed. "What else could go wrong?" thought Patty.

Chapter 4

On the Back of a Motorcycle

Finally, the rain eased. The sound of an engine could be heard humming in the distance. Patty was the first to hear it.

"It's a car, I think," she said excitedly.

"Run!" cried Cousin Fiona.

Patty sprinted to the road and waved her arms frantically. She could see two dots . . . no, three, in the distance. They weren't cars. They were motorcycles.

Three shiny motorcycles pulled up in front of Patty. She swallowed hard as the three leather-clad riders jumped off their bikes.

"Looks like you need help," the oldest rider said. "We're going to a wedding, but we've got time to help you." Then he looked at Cousin Fiona in surprise. "Don't tell me you're the bride!"

The three motorcyclists were friends of the groom. Cousin Fiona was so relieved to see friendly faces and find a reliable form of transportation, that she didn't mind hopping on the back of a motorcycle to ride to her wedding.

When they were almost at the church, Cousin Fiona signaled everyone to stop.

"I can't go into the church like this. Look at me! My dress is torn and all muddy from my knees down." Tears began to roll down her cheeks.

Patty knew she was right. Although the wind had dried their clothes, the dresses were ruined. Cousin Fiona's dress was ripped and torn. Her own dress was shredded along the sleeves, and Uncle Stuart looked like a scarecrow!

"Don't worry," Patty told her cousin. "We'll think of something."

Cousin Fiona grinned and took Patty's hand. "I should have picked you for my bridesmaid in the first place," she said. "It's just that your mom said you didn't like dressing up or meeting people—but you've been so patient and kind. I just want you to know that I appreciate it."

Patty realized then that it wasn't so bad to dress up for a day. It had been the most exciting day of her life.

"I've got an idea," Patty began, as she looked at the golden carpet of flowers in the nearby field. "If you'd like to look really cool, that is, and you're not allergic to flowers."

Cousin Fiona was desperate. She agreed to Patty's idea, even though it was going to shock the guests and her husband-to-be!

Chapter 5

Here Comes the Bride

They roared up to the church just an hour
late, on three shiny motorcycles.

"These modern brides," Patty heard an older lady mutter, as they walked down the aisle. "They don't wear traditional dresses anymore."

The bride and bridesmaid wore similar outfits—short, trendy satin dresses that looked more like slips than bridal-party dresses. The father-of-the-bride wore black leather pants and a black leather jacket with a bow tie. As for the flowers—there were wildflower bouquets, wildflowers in the girls' hair, and wildflowers in Uncle Stuart's lapel.

Everyone, including Patty's mother, stared in amazement as the bridal party arrived at the altar.

Fiona's husband-to-be beamed at his bride.

"This is going to be the talk of the town for a very long time," Patty's mother whispered to Patty. "And you've done such a good job of not being shy in front of so many people!"

Patty smiled. She wondered if her mom would actually believe that she was the mastermind behind the fashionable wedding dress. Would she be shocked to know that her shy daughter had cut up the satin slips and made them into dresses?

It was going to be hard to convince her twin sister, Penny, that she, Patty, had actually saved the day with her brilliant ideas. But Patty didn't care. If she could survive Cousin Fiona's disastrous wedding, she could survive anything—including reading aloud in class and being the center of attention!

About the Author

Rose Inserra

Rose Inserra was a high school teacher before she became a children's author. She loves to write funny stories, and her two daughters, Melinda and Andrea, provide her with many amusing plots.

Trixie the cat and Ginger the dog keep her company during the day, along with cockatoos and blue-tongued lizards, while she writes her books.

The idea for a disastrous wedding day came from attending many large family weddings. There was usually a disaster of some kind, but everything always worked out in the end. Well, almost always!

About the Illustrator

Trish Hill

Trish studied fine arts, specializing in printmaking and drawing. She has illustrated many books, and she tries to use a different medium each time.

In between illustrating, Trish is busy being a mom—but sometimes, she does forget to hang out the laundry or feed the cat. Fortunately, she hardly ever forgets to feed the family! Trish loves to play tennis and read; her latest passion is golf.

Trish lives in Melbourne, Australia, with her husband and two children.